WITHDRA

ARCHIE'S VACATION

First published as *Archie's Holiday* in Great Britain in August 2013 by Bloomsbury Publishing Plc
Published in the United States of America in March 2014 by Bloomsbury Children's Books
www.bloomsbury.com

For information about permission to reproduce selections from this book, write to
Permissions, Bloomsbury Children's Books, 1385 Broadway, New York, New York 10018
Bloomsbury books may be purchased for business or promotional use. For information on bulk purchases please
contact Macmillan Corporate and Premium Sales Department at specialmarkets@macmillan.com

Library of Congress Cataloging-in-Publication Data
available upon request
ISBN 978-1-61963-190-8 (hardcover) • ISBN 978-1-61963-191-5 (reinforced)

Art created with mixed media
Hand lettering created by Domenica More Gordon

Printed in China by C&C Offset Printing Co., Ltd., Shenzhen, Guangdong
2 4 6 8 10 9 7 5 3 1 (hardcover)
2 4 6 8 10 9 7 5 3 1 (reinforced)

ARCHIE'S
VACATION

Domenica More Gordon

BLOOMSBURY

NEW YORK LONDON NEW DELHI SYDNEY

HAIL?
RAIN? SNOW?
HURRICANES?
LIGHTNING?
THUNDER?
WATERPROO
LONG, THICK, WOOL
MORE SOCKS
YIKES!
FREEZIN
NO!

VITAMINS FOR EVERYTHING!
BLUE AND RED VITAMINS, COUGH DROPS
ALL POSSIBLE TYPES OF CREAM!
JELLYFISH STING CREAM
BIG VITAMINS
ICE PACKS
ANTI-SNAKE VENOM STUFF
MORE CREAM
PHEW!
ALLERGIES?
HELP!
CREAM
THAT'S BETTER!

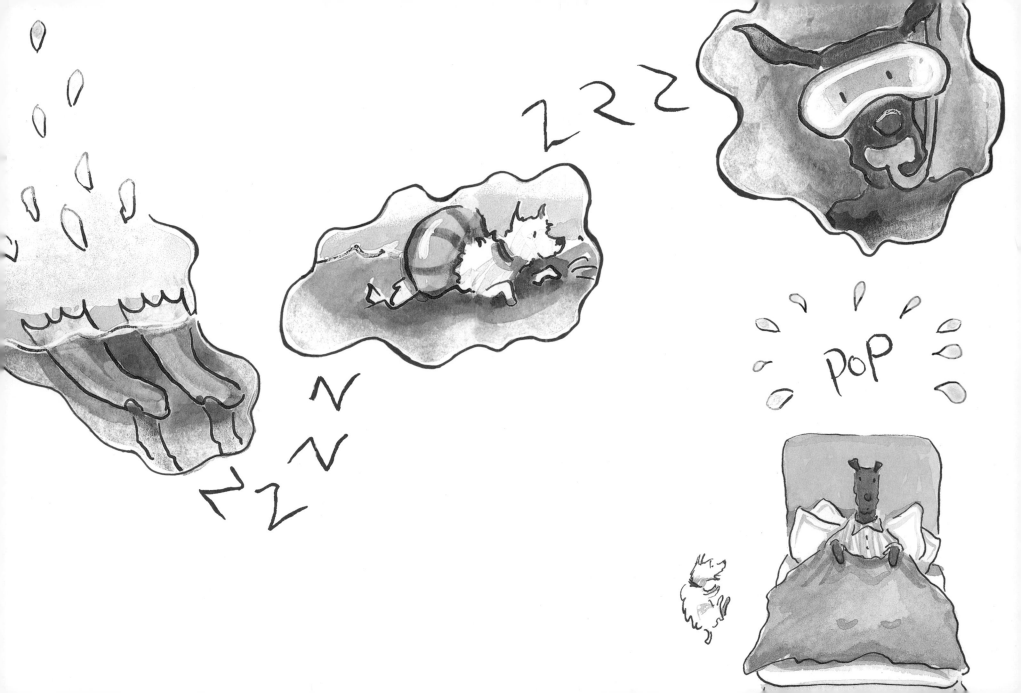

DECK CHAIRS x 2

BLOW-UP LOCH NESS MONSTER

SHARK CAGE!

EXTRA TRUNKS

SUBMARINE?

SHOVEL

FRYING PAN

FLOATIES

SWIMMING CAPS x 2

WET SUITS

PIRAT?

WINDSURFER ? BAT

THE WONDERFUL WORLD OF SHELLS

WINDBREAKE

FAKE SHARK FIN

COOLER

KNOW YOUR SEAWEED BOOK

CANOE?

CRICKET BAT

BEACH BAG

SNORKELS + 2

FISH?

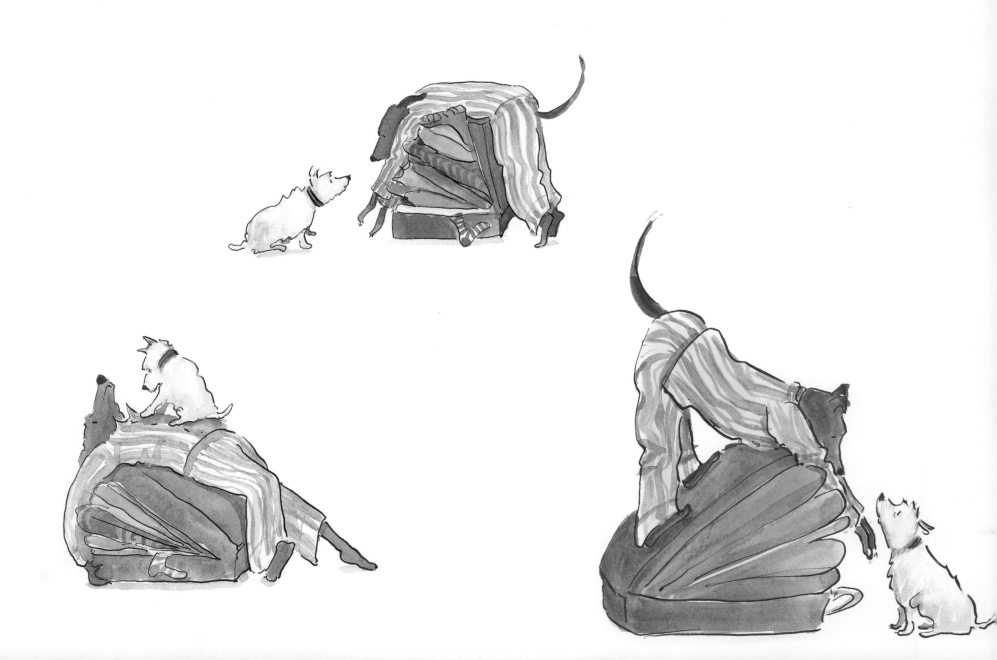

CREEEAK

BA

NG!

BARK
BARK
BARK

SUN, SEA, SAND
YIPPEE TRA-LAAAA,
GOOD BOOKS FUN
SUNTAN
PEACE

HERE WE COME!
HOORAY
WAHOO!
ICE CREAM
VACATIONS FOREVER!
NEW FRIENDS
NEW THOUGHTS
NEW ME!

Wish you were here!
— ARCHIE XOXO